Ghosts

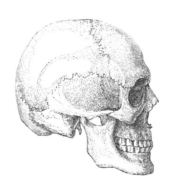

Ghosts

A COLLECTION OF SPIRITS FROM LITERATURE AND FOLKLORE

Abbie Headon

First published in 2025

Copyright © 2025 Amber Books Ltd

All rights reserved. No part of this publication may be reproduced, stored in a retrieval system, or transmitted in any form or by any means, electronic, mechanical, photocopying, recording, or otherwise, without prior written permission of the copyright holder.

Published by
Amber Books Ltd
United House
London N7 9DP
United Kingdom
www.amberbooks.co.uk
Facebook: amberbooks
YouTube: amberbooksltd
Instagram: amberbooksltd
X(Twitter): @amberbooks

ISBN: 978-1-83886-599-3

Project Editor: Anna Brownbridge
Designer: Keren Harragan
Picture Research: Terry Forshaw

Printed in China

Contents

Introduction	6
Ghosts from Folklore	
Adze	10
Amadlozi	12
Asanbosam	14
Egbere	16
Madam Koi Koi	18
Mbwiri	20
Obambo	22
Obayifo	24
Obia	26
Ogbanje	28
Tokoloshe	30
Wangliang	32
Ayakashi	34
Lantern Ghost, Japan	36
Hungry Ghosts, Japan	38
Ghosts of the Philippines	40
Dullahan	42
Stingy Jack	44
The Wild Hunt	46
The White Lady	48
Bloody Mary	50
La Llorona	52
La Sayona	54
Myling	56
Fylgia	58
Genius loci	60
Shade	62
Vrykolakas	64
Historical Ghosts	
Agnes Sampson	68
The Brown Lady	70
Banff Springs Hotel ghosts	72
Scratching Fanny	74
The Drummer of Tedworth	76
The Ghost Nun of Borley Rectory	78
Marie Laveau, the Voodoo Queen	80
The Ghosts of the Dakota, New York	82
The Man in Grey, Theatre Royal	84
Marie Antoinette	86
The Ghosts of 10 Downing St	88
Annie Morgan	90
Nan Tuck's Ghost	92
Fisher's Ghost	94
Napoleon	96
Monte Cristo Homestead	98
Resurrection Mary	100
The Ghosts of Anchorage Hotel	102
Queen Esther	104
The Ghosts of the Battle of Gettysburg	106
Anne Boleyn	108
The Grey Lady, Bolsover Castle	110
The Green Lady, Château de Brissac	112
The Blue Boy, Chillingham Castle	114
Alice and Felix, Château de Fougeret	116
Spinning Jenny, Knebworth House	118
The Grey Lady, Glamis Castle	120
Pausanias of Sparta	122
El Cid	124
Ghosts from Literature	
Armida	128
The Ghost of Hamlet's father	130
Banquo's Ghost	132
The Headless Horseman	134
The Flying Dutchman	136
The Ghosts from A Christmas Carol	138
The Canterville Ghost	140
Miss Jessel and Peter Quint	142
The 'ghost' of Rebecca	144
Casper the Friendly Ghost	146
The Dead Men of Dunharrow	148
The Overlook Hotel	150
The Ghost of Beloved	152
Slimer	154
The Hogwarts Ghosts	156
Susie Salmon	158
Picture Credits	160

Introduction

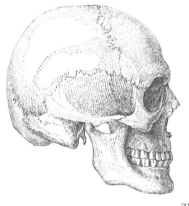

As a traditional prayer cries out, 'From ghoulies and ghosties and long-leggedy beasties, and things that go bump in the night, Good Lord, deliver us!'

This little guide to the ghosts of the world's folklore, history and arts takes the opposite approach. Instead of trying to avoid the scary side of the supernatural world, we are diving into it headfirst.

We will discover a cast of wild and rage-filled child-snatchers, creatures who can divide themselves in half or remove their own heads, vengeful spouses and many more. Whether you believe in these ghosts or not, one thing is certain: the human imagination can create an infinite number of terrors, and delights in exploring everything that goes beyond the reach of rational explanation.

Ghosts from Folklore

Cultures around the world have different traditions and ways of viewing the world, but one element that seems to be present in every folklore is a belief in supernatural forces that can threaten, help or control us.

In this chapter we will meet shapeshifters and vampires, child stealers, vengeful spouses, benevolent spirits that accompany us through life and malign entities who are all too eager to drain our life and energy as soon as our guard is down.

Enter into the world of folklore – but watch out for ghouls in human clothing…

Ghosts of humans, animals and other entities are found in almost every culture round the world.

Adze

No matter how tightly you lock your doors at night, there are some intruders who simply cannot be kept out, and the Adze is one of these. According to the traditional folklore of the Ewe people of Ghana and Togo, the Adze is a malicious vampiric spirit that takes the form of a firefly in the wild, making it small enough to slip into any home. A human who is bitten by an Adze is at risk of losing their life, and the Adze's malevolent spirit can be manifested by the host bringing misfortune to other members of the family, in the form of jealousy, bitterness or ill health.

Once upon a time…
The Adze's wild form as an insect that can infiltrate people's homes to cause pain and damage may be related to the all-too-real presence of mosquitos that carry diseases such as malaria.

Origins:
The Adze is a vampiric being in the folklore of the Ewe people of Ghana and Togo.

In popular culture:
The Adze is featured in museum displays in Ghana, to give visitors an insight into a unique cultural tradition.

The haunting bite of the Adze could herald the arrival of malaria in the home.

"Suffering and happiness are twins."

– Ewe proverb

*"It is indeed a desirable thing
to be well descended, but the glory
belongs to our ancestors."*

– *Plutarch*

In the Nguni culture, ancestors return to guide their descendants as Amadlozi.

Amadlozi

In many traditions, those who have gone before us have not disappeared, but remain present in our lives to guide and comfort us. The Nguni culture of southern Africa celebrates Amadlozi, ancestral spirits who provide the wisdom of the past to those living today. Amadlozi may take the shape of a human, or may make their presence known in a more intangible way, such as a cool breeze, a warm wind or a sense of sudden stillness. Although they can be tricksters, they usually exert a positive influence, guiding their loved ones to a life of integrity and purpose. They only lose their power when they are forgotten by their community, breaking the threads between the present day and past generations.

Once upon a time…
The word 'Amadlozi' comes from Zulu and Xhosa, and translates as 'spirits' or 'shades'.

Origins:
Amadlozi are ancestral spirits in the tradition of the Nguni peoples of southern Africa.

In popular culture:
Christianity co-exists with the cultural presence of Amadlozi in Southern Africa, particularly in Zulu-speaking communities.

Asanbosam

he Asanbosam, also known as the Sasanbosam, is one of the most terrifying creatures in any folkloric tradition. It dwells in the abundant forests of west Africa, and resembles a bat – but this is no ordinary bat. It has glowing red eyes in a pink human-like face, skinny limbs, long hooked talons which enable it to cling to tree branches, and teeth made of iron. Most shockingly, it is huge and fast, with a wingspan of up to 6m (20ft). Anyone who wanders into the forest at night could become the Asanbosam's next victim, passing unknowingly by its home in a hollow silk-cotton tree. The Asanbosam moves silently and swiftly, bewitching anyone it meets and draining them of their precious blood.

Once upon a time…
The collections of the British Museum hold a wooden sculpture from 1935 that depicts an Asanbosam with horns, wings and looped legs.

Origins:
The Asanbosam is a vampiric being from the folklore of the Akan people of Côte d'Ivoire, Togo, southern Ghana and 18th century Jamaica.

In popular culture:
References to the Asanbosam extend beyond its west African origins, and it can be found in video games and other works of fiction around the world as an embodiment of terror.

The nightmarish Asanbosam is huge, fast-moving and deadly to anyone who encounters it.

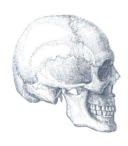

"Blood is a juice of rarest quality."

– *Johann Wolfgang von Goethe* , Faust: A Tragedy

Egbere

oney brings comfort and ease to our lives, but the quest to acquire it can often be painful, with negative consequences. In Yoruba mythology, the forests of Nigeria are home to a small human-like figure called the Egbere, who wanders sadly and endlessly, weeping like a baby and holding onto a rolled-up mat. Anyone who can successfully steal the Egbere's mat will be rewarded with great wealth, but to hold onto it, they will have to endure the Egbere's plaintive crying outside their window, night after night. Eventually, the Egbere will lose its strength and fade away, leaving the mat-holder with the fortune they desired – but the emotional strain of ignoring the Egbere's grief will leave its mark on them forever.

Once upon a time…
One legend surrounding the creation of the Egbere is that it sprang from the soul of a miserly rich person, who is now condemned to roam with a small mat as its only possession.

Origins:
The Egbere is a small malevolent spirit in the Yoruba people in west Africa, spanning the countries of Nigeria, Togo and Benin.

In popular culture:
The word 'egbere' is sometimes used as a swear word in Yoruba society by older people towards irritating and bothersome youngsters.

*If you can steal the Egbere's mat, you will find fortune
— but at a terrble price.*

"It is not the man who has too little, but the man who craves more, that is poor."

– *Seneca*

"It is the woman whose child has been eaten by a witch who best knows the evils of witchcraft."

– *Nigerian proverb*

Madame Koi Koi is believed to haunt children in Nigerian boarding schools.

Madam Koi Koi

It is well-known that Hell hath no fury like a woman scorned – and when that woman is a teacher, it is her pupils who are forced to suffer the consequences. Madam Koi Koi is a creature of urban legend in Nigeria, a teacher who lost her job in unfortunate circumstances and subsequently died in poverty. From the afterlife, she takes her revenge on schoolchildren in boarding schools, slapping them and attacking them in toilets and bathrooms. She can be heard whistling and singing, and she is always accompanied by the click of her stylish red shoes tapping along the floor with a distinctive 'koi koi' sound.

Once upon a time…
Madam Koi Koi's name is derived from the sounds of her high-heeled shoes tapping along the corridors of a boarding school.

Origins:
Madam Koi Koi is a character from urban legend who haunts the toilets, dormitories and hallways of Nigerian boarding schools.

In popular culture:
The myth of Madam Koi Koi was made into a two-part horror film by Netflix, broadcast in 2023, with the title *The Origin: Madam Koi-Koi*.

Mbwiri

he Mbwiri does not have a physical form, but is a spirit that can take over the mind and body of an innocent person. It cannot be seen, it is perceived by the impact it has on those it encounters, sowing conflict and strife. People possessed by the Mbwiri may suffer from uncontrollable shaking, in a way that would be diagnosed as an epileptic fit in medical terms. Although the Mbwiri is dangerous, it can sometimes give powers to the person it possesses, such as exceptional strength or the ability to speak in unknown languages.

Once upon a time...
The Mbwiri may be an ancient demon stemming from the creation of the universe, or possibly the spirit of a sorcerer who was wronged in life and now seeks vengeance.

Origins:
The Mbwiri is a demonic spirit that can possess people, according to the tradition of the Fang people of central Africa.

In popular culture:
A traditional technique for exorcising a Mbwiri is for the possessed person staying in a specially constructed hut with a shaman until the possession has ended.

The Mbwiri can only be seen through its effects on the people it possesses.

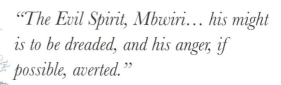

"The Evil Spirit, Mbwiri… his might is to be dreaded, and his anger, if possible, averted."

– *W.H. Davenport Adams*, Witch, Warlock, and Magician

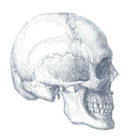

"Ghosts are all around us. Look for them, and you will find them."

– *Ruskin Bond*

When a person dies alone in the wilderness, their spirit may return as an Obambo.

Obambo

n uneasy spirit stalks the bush and jungle of central Africa: the Obambo, said to be the ghost of someone who died in the wilderness and was never buried. When it wearies of its lonely wandering, an Obambo may approach populated areas and take possession of an innocent person, dwelling in their victim's bowels and causing them great distress. One way to try to lift the spirit's curse is to sing, dance and make as much noise as possible around the affected person, to drive the Obambo out. Another strategy is to make a small figurine representing the dead person and then bury it, enabling them to find peace and cease their possession of the victim.

Once upon a time...
According to the traditions of the Commi tribe, an Obambo could be the reason for the illness of a member of their community.

Origins:
An Obambo is an evil spirit from central Africa that can possess people and make them sick.

In popular culture:
A horror film titled *Obambo*, written and directed by Freddy Feruzi, was released in 2022.

Obayifo

According to the folklore of the Ashanti, an obayifo is a creature somewhat like a vampire, who feeds on other people's despair and fear, sucking out the life-force of their victims. People are born with the innate tendency to be an obayifo, meaning that it is not a status that can be caught or transferred to someone else. An obayifo's skin emits light when they are in motion, or when they are threatened with violence, with the light emerging rather disconcertingly from their armpits and anus. If they eat or drink certain foods, such as cacao beans or a special elixir, they can gain other powers including shapeshifting and flight.

Once upon a time…
In the Twi language, the word 'bayi' is used to describe witchcraft, with 'obayifo' meaning a person who practises witchcraft.

Origins:
The obayifo is a vampire-like creature from the Ashanti folklore of west Africa.

In popular culture:
The 2024 horror film *Obayifo Project* tells the story of a group of filmmakers who attempt to recreate an obayifo-raising experiment from years earlier.

Drawn to the despair of others, the Obayifo feeds on its victims with a vampiric appetite.

"An obayifo in everyday life is supposed to be known by having sharp, shifty eyes that are never at rest."

– *Montague Summers*, The Vampire, His Kith and Kin

"The dead man says, 'What you are, I have been, what I am you are yet to be.'"

— *Igbo proverb*

Feared by communities, the Obia is believed to steal young girls and wear their skins.

Obia

The obia is a terrifying entity in west African folklore, a huge creature that is sent into villages by witches to steal young girls. It then takes the skin of its victim and wears it like a coat. The word 'obia' can also refer to a wider concept of a supernatural power that connects the worlds of the living and the dead. In the Caribbean, particularly in Jamaica, the term 'obeah' has a broad meaning covering healing and spell-casting traditional practices. It is still widely practised today, despite laws dating back to the 18th century making it illegal, and its popularity has grown in the post-colonial era.

Once upon a time...
The term 'obiama' or 'obiman' is used to describe someone who can use the power of obia.

Origins:
In west African folklore, an obia is a huge animal that is sent into villages by witches to steal young girls.

In popular culture:
Popular musicians have used the word 'obeah' in the names of songs such as 'Obeah Wedding' by Mighty Sparrows, from Trinidad, and 'Obeah Book' by The Ethiopians, from Jamaica.

Ogbanje

Supernatural beliefs often speak to our fears and griefs, and the ogbanje – meaning 'children who come and go' in the Igbo language – do this at the deepest level. Ogbanje are evil spirits who curse a family by inhabiting a small child, then deliberately dying, only to be reincarnated in the next child to be born to the family. This cycle brings immense grief, and may have been a way for communities to give a narrative to the unexplained deaths of small children due to unknown diseases. One way of breaking an ogbanje's curse is to locate and destroy its Iyi-uwa, a stone that acts as an anchor, enabling it to return to its targeted family.

Once upon a time…
The concept of a child who has been replaced by a supernatural being is common in many folklore traditions, for example in the changelings in European mythologies.

Origins:
According to Odinani cultural practices in southeast and south south Nigeria, an ogbanje is an evil spirt that reincarnates repeatedly in infants.

In popular culture:
Ogbanjes have been featured in many novels, such as *Things Fall Apart* by Chinua Achebe and *Freshwater* by Akwaeke Emezi.

The Ogbanje may exist in folklore as a way to explain the deaths of infants.

"A dead person shall have all the sleep necessary."

– *Igbo proverb*

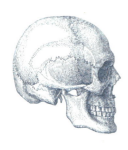

"'Keep the heart of the chicken with you so the tokoloshe does not follow you home,' the nyanga's voice advises in Zulu."

– *Bill Keller, 'Johannesburg Journal',* The New York Times, *8 August 1992*

Nobody is safe in bed at night when a Tokoloshe comes to call.

Tokoloshe

It's not always easy to find a restful night's sleep, and according to Zulu mythology, an extra night-time worry comes in the form of the tokoloshe, a creature that attacks sleepers in their beds. They are described as small, gremlin-sized humans, sometimes with gouged-out holes where their eyes should be. In their evil acts, tokoloshes can scare their victims, leave them covered in scratches or even choke them to death. A traditional healer, known as a sangoma, can set a tokoloshe upon someone else for a fee, or exorcise one from a victim's home. One strategy to stay safe from them is to place a stack of bricks under each leg of a person's bed.

Once upon a time…
The connection between a raised bed and the avoidance of deaths at night may be because when people slept at floor level, they were more at risk of carbon monoxide poisoning.

Origins:
The tokoloshe is a trouble-making water spirit in Nguni mythology, which can be called upon to hurt someone else.

In popular culture:
In 1971 John Kongos's 'Tokoloshe Man' became a hit single in the UK, and it was later released as a cover version by the Happy Mondays.

Wangliang

he wangliang is a demon from Chinese folklore that is known and feared for its supernatural powers and cunning. Some wangliangs are based in a particular natural setting, such as water spirits or wood spirits. Another type of wangliang is a human-shaped demon the size of a small child, with red skin, hair and claws. Some of them eat the brains of dead people, or attack the living. Sometimes they may be driven by mischief rather than evil, but it is wise to keep out of their way, as meeting a wangliang may lead to sickness, madness or even death.

Once upon a time...
The earliest known mention of the wangliang is found in the *Discourses of the States*, dating to the 5th–4th century BCE.

Origins:
The wangliang is a malevolent Chinese spirit that may be found in water, wild places or graveyards.

In popular culture:
The novel *Let Me Game in Peace* by Twelve-Winged Dark Seraphim contains wangliangs whose bodies are made of black liquid, which can splatter and reform at will.

Wangliangs come in many physical forms, but their acts are always destructive.

"The appearance of the wangliang is like that of a three-year-old child, with a red-black color, red eyes, long ears and beautiful hair."

– *Xu Shen*, Shuowen jiezi

Ayakashi

In Japanese, the word 'yōkai' describes strange apparitions, and those that appear on the surface of water are known as 'ayakashi'. In legends from the Nagasaki, Yamaguchi and Saga prefectures, ayakashi appear as ghostly lights dancing on the surface of the sea. These lights can resemble rocks or mountains that threaten to dash a boat to pieces, but a brave captain who steers directly towards them will come through safely. Another ayakashi tale by the 18th century writer Toriyama Sekien concerns a giant sea serpent that slithers over a ship for days, dripping with oil that the sailors had to bail out in order to avoid drowning.

Once upon a time…
In an Edo-period legend, an ayakashi appears as a ghostly woman who brought water to a boat; when the boat put to sea, she pursued it and bit into its hull.

Origins:
In the natural world, ayakashi are associated with the remora, or suckerfish, which uses a sucker to attach itself to bigger creatures, and sometimes even to boats.

In popular culture:
In the manga and anime series *Noragami*, ayakashi are supernatural creatures that can influence humans.

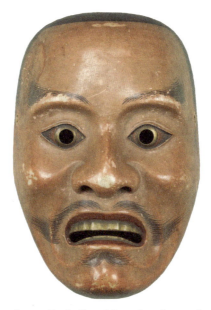

As well as watching the tides and the weather, sailors must beware of the dangerous Ayakashi.

"…all the sea sparkles to the horizon with the lights of the dead, and the sea wind is fragrant with incense."

– *Lafcardio Hearn*, Glimpses of Unfamiliar Japan: First Series

"Splitting apart the lantern set out during the Festival of the Dead (Bon Matsuri) the ghost of O'Iwa appears with the child in her embrace."

– *James S. de Benneville,* The Yotsuya Kwaidan or O'iwa Inari

*Oiwa, cruelly tricked and murdered by her husband,
returned to haunt him on a paper lantern.*

Lantern Ghost

he Lantern Ghost is one of Japan's most enduring ghost stories. It was launched to fame in a 19th century play by Tsuruya Nanboku IV, but its roots go back as far as 1784 when it appears in a demonology. Nanboku's play tells the story of a woman called Oiwa, whose husband Iemon wants to marry his neighbour's granddaughter. Iemon gives Oiwa poisoned face cream that disfigures her, and she eventually kills herself, cursing him with her dying breath. Oiwa haunts her unfaithful husband, causing him to kill his new bride and her father, and appears to him in the form of a burning paper lantern. With his death, Oiwa's vengeance is complete.

Once upon a time…
In Japan, it is traditional to tell ghost stories by lantern light in the summertime, in contrast to the European Halloween of 31st October.

Origins:
The most famous lantern ghost is a woman called Oiwa, who was poisoned by her husband, killed herself and returned on a paper lantern to haunt him.

In popular culture:
The story of the lantern ghost first appeared on stage in the kabuki theatres of Edo (now Tokyo), in a play known as Yotsuya Kaidan, and influences Japanese horror writing to this day.

Hungry Ghosts

In Buddhist cosmology there are six realms of existence: gods, demi-gods, humans, animals, hungry ghosts and beings in hell. When a human dies, they will be reborn into one of these realms, and those whose lives were sinful but not evil enough to go to hell become hungry ghosts, forced to wander the earth with the living, driven by an insatiable appetite. The two main types are the *gaki*, who hunger and thirst for something humiliating, like human excrement, or something they cannot eat because their mouths are too small, and the *jikininki*, who are driven to eat human flesh. The ritual of *segaki*, meaning 'feeding the hungry ghosts' is done by humans in the hope of releasing them from their torment.

Once upon a time…
Hungry ghosts appear in the Buddhist traditions of many countries, including China, Tibet, Cambodia and Japan.

Origins:
Hungry ghosts arise when a person committed sins in life which are not bad enough to condemn them to hell, but which prevent reincarnation into a new life.

In popular culture:
Japan's three-day-long Obon festival in late summer or early autumn is based on the principle of honouring ancestral spirits.

Hungry ghosts wander the earth in misery, driven by their insatiable appetites.

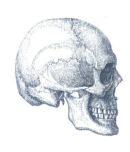

"At sunset on the evening of the 15th only the offerings called Segaki are made in the temples."

– *Lafcardio Hearn,* Glimpses of Unfamiliar Japan: First Series

"The seventh was called magtatangal, and his purpose was to show himself at night to many persons, without his head or entrails."

– *Fr. Juan de Plasencia*, Customs of the Tagalogs

One of the most terrifying ghosts of the Philippines is the Manananggal, whose upper half can fly.

Ghosts of the Philippines

With a population of over 114 million and over 100 regional languages, the Philippines has a good supply of supernatural creatures. The Aswang is a shapeshifter who may be a vampire, witch or ghoul who feasts on dead flesh. The Kapre is a tall and hairy human-like creature found sitting under trees in which they dwell. If you meet a Manananggal, you will be shocked by how it can separate its upper and lower body, the head, arms and torso can fly like a vampire. And you must harden your heart against the Tiyanak, a goblin that disguises itself as a baby in order to trick people into carrying it into their homes.

Once upon a time...
There are over 182 ethnolinguistic groups in the Philippines, giving rise to a richly diverse cast of legendary and mythological characters.

Origins:
Philippine mythologies offer a vast range of gods, heroes, monsters – and ghosts.

In popular culture:
The ghosts of Philippine culture have provided inspiration for countless films, such as the horror films *Manananggal* of 1927 and *Maria Labo* of 2015.

Dullahan

he Dullahan of Irish folklore feels like the creation of a fever dream: he rides through the night on horseback, carrying his own head, which is shaped like a giant wheel of cheese and which he can place back on his neck or kick around like a football. His grin, filled with razor-like teeth, stretches to the sides of his head, and his eyes dart around like flies. In a variation of this tale, the Dullahan is not a rider but the coachman of a carriage made of bones and pulled by six headless horses. Meeting a Dullahan on the road is a bad omen – and whatever happens, seems sure to leave any viewer with nightmares for the rest of their life.

Once upon a time…
In Irish, the Dullahan is known as the *Dubhlachan*, signifying a dark or sullen person.

Origins:
According to Irish legend, the Dullahan is a headless horseman, or the coachman of a carriage who carries his own head in his hands.

In popular culture:
Headless horsemen are found in many European folktales, dating back to the medieval period. The Sleepy Hollow High School in Westchester, New York, even has one as its school mascot.

Try not to lose your head if you meet the Dullahan riding through the forest at night.

"*By the big bridge of Mallow, it is no head at all he has!*"

– T. *Crofton Crocker*, Fairy Legends and Traditions of the South of Ireland

43

*"Then since Jack is unfit for heaven,
And hell won't give him room,
His ghost is forced to walk the earth
Until the day of doom"*

– *Hercules Ellis,* The Romance of Jack O'Lantern

*Is Stingy Jack real or a parable against meanness?
Best to buy the next round just in case.*

Stingy Jack

In Irish legend, Stingy Jack was a drunkard whose favourite pastime was cheating people. One day, the Devil came to take him away, but Jack tricked him into becoming a coin, which he put in his pocket with a crucifix. The frustrated Devil agreed to give Jack 10 years on earth in return for his freedom. When the Devil returned, Jack tricked him again, and he bargained successfully that he would never enter Hell. However, when Jack died, he was barred from Heaven because of his bad deeds and from Hell because of the Devil's promise. His fate, then, was to wander the world forever, with only a carved turnip lamp to light the way.

Once upon a time…
The *Dublin Penny Journal* published a story in 1836 in which an angel offered Stingy Jack three wishes but was so disappointed by his mean requests that he was stopped from entering Heaven.

Origins:
Stingy Jack is a character from Irish folklore who, as a result of his own trickery, was unable to enter Heaven or Hell and had to roam among the living forever.

In popular culture:
Stingy Jack's turnip lantern evolved into the pumpkin form we know today, and still bears his name: the Jack O'Lantern.

The Wild Hunt

he countryside at nighttime is the perfect setting for dark imaginings to run free, and that is what happens with the legend of the Wild Hunt, which can be found throughout Europe. In every version of the story, a pack of bloodthirsty hunters rampages across the land led by a powerful figure such as Odin, the Devil or a famous king. The first written occurrence of the legend can be found in the Anglo-Saxon Chronicle in 1127. The chronicler relates that several people saw a pack of huntsmen on horseback ride through the city of Peterborough to Stamford, and that their shouting and horn-blowing was heard by monks throughout the night.

Once upon a time…
The concept of the Wild hunt can be found across many European folklore traditions, particularly in German, Celtic and Slavic mythologies.

Origins:
The Wild Hunt is a legend telling of a powerful mythological figure leading a pack of phantom animals in a chase through the countryside.

In popular culture:
In a cinematically sized canvas of 1872, the Norwegian artist Peter Nicolai Arbo painted an epic scene of *The Wild Hunt of Odin*, with hunters and Valkyries galloping across a stormy sky on horseback.

The Wild Hunt has fascinated chroniclers and artists for centuries.

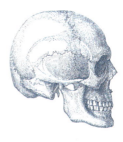

"The hunters were swarthy, and huge, and ugly; and their hounds were all swarthy, and broad-eyed, and ugly."

– *The Anglo-Saxon Chronicle, entry for CE 1127*

The White Lady

erhaps it is because history is overflowing with stories of the mistreatment of women that there are so many ghosts who take the form of a white lady. Whether she has been abandoned at the altar, walled up and left to die or been murdered, the white lady roams through the subconscious minds all over the world. Sometimes she is based on a historical figure, such as Lady Mary Howard of Fitzford House in Devon, who was widowed three times and now rides through the countryside in a carriage made of the bones of her dead husbands. In other legends the white lady's roots are unknown – but in all cases, her appearance signals misfortune.

Once upon a time…
In Britain, the legend of the white lady stretches to pre-Roman times, to protective goddesses who were often associated with life-giving springs.

Origins:
The white lady is an archetypal ghost who appears in many folklore traditions all over the world, usually signifying a tragic omen.

In popular culture:
Although not strictly a ghost story, Wilkie Collins' novel *The Woman in White* has a mysterious white-robed woman at its heart, and has been adapted for stage and screen ever since its publication in 1860.

The spectral figure of a White Lady occurs frequently in the history of folklore.

"My ladye's coach hath nodding plumes,
The driver hath no head;
My ladye is an ashen white,
As one that long is dead."

– Lady Howard's Coach

"Whence and what are thou, execrable shape?"

– *John Milton,* Paradise Lost

Who knows what future secrets might you discover if you call upon Bloody Mary?

Bloody Mary

 one of us knows what the future holds, but those who call on Bloody Mary hope for a chance to have their questions answered. According to folklore, if you call her name a certain number of times under the right conditions, Bloody Mary will appear in the mirror in front of you as a ghost or demon. She is also referred to as Hell Mary or Mary Worth in some quarters. One explanation for the popularity of this legend is the Troxler Effect, first named in 1804: the tendency of the brain to invent additional phenomena when a person stares into a mirror for a prolonged period.

Once upon a time…
Queen Mary I of England was also given the nickname 'Bloody Mary' in reference to the hundreds of Protestants who were executed during her reign.

Origins:
Bloody Mary is the name of an apparition who can be summoned by looking in a mirror and chanting her name repeatedly.

In popular culture:
Beyond the ghost world, a Bloody Mary is a spicy red cocktail, composed of vodka and tomato juice, and seasoned with Worcestershire sauce, Tabasco, salt and pepper.

La Llorona

La Llorona, the weeping woman, appears throughout Latin American folklore. In one version, she is the ghost of a mother who drowned her children in a rage after discovering that her husband had been unfaithful to her. In other variations, her husband favoured her sons while treating her abusively, or she neglected her sons and they drowned accidentally. In every case, she now cries endlessly, and anyone who hears her is likely to suffer misfortune. Her tale has been told to children to keep them from roaming in the dark or playing close to lakes without supervision, and recently she has also become a symbol of how women can be driven beyond breaking point by cruel treatment.

Once upon a time...
The legend of La Llorona dates back to 16th century Mexico, and may be connected to ancient Aztec creation myths.

Origins:
The name 'La Llorona' means 'the weeping woman', describes the sorrow of a woman who drowned her own children in a jealous rage.

In popular culture:
La Llorona has featured in numerous films from the 1930s to the present day, including *The Curse of the Crying Woman* (1963), *Mulholland Drive* (2001) and *The Legend of La Llorona* (2022).

The ghost La Llorona weeps unceasingly for the children she drowned in a jealous rage.

"Ghost stories ... tell us about things that lie hidden within all of us, and which lurk outside all around us."

– Susan Hill, Ghost stories

La Sayona

A shocking Venezuelan legend tells the story of La Sayona, a beautiful woman who once enjoyed a happy home with her husband and baby. Her fortunes changed when a man saw her bathing one day and told her that her beloved husband was having an affair with her mother. Incensed with rage, La Sayona ran home and burned down the house containing her husband and their child. She then attacked her mother, cutting her stomach open with a machete. As punishment for her crimes, La Sayona was condemned to wander forever more, in search of unfaithful men who she would tempt into the jungle with her beauty before mauling them to death.

Once upon a time...
La Sayona's name refers to the simple white garment that she wears, and can be translated roughly as 'the woman in sackcloth'.

Origins:
In Venezuelan legend, La Sayona is the spirit of a woman who haunts men who are unfaithful to their wives.

In popular culture:
Tales about the vengeance of angry women are found throughout history in all cultures, from Medea in 431 BCE to Amy Dunne in *Gone Girl*.

La Sayona, driven in life to desperate acts, now roams in search of unfaithful husbands to punish.

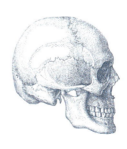

"An angry woman is vindictive beyond measure, and hesitates at nothing in her bitterness."

– Jean Antoine Petit-Senn

"Fear the reckoning of those you have wronged."

– 'Hávamál'

In Scandinavian folklore, a myling is the ghost of a child who was not given a proper burial.

Myling

he myling is one of the most tragic and terrifying ghosts in Scandinavian folklore. According to legend, a myling is the soul of an infant who was not given the correct funeral rites, perhaps because it was born out of wedlock and buried in secret. These tormented spirits roam in search of someone who can help them find peace, by giving them either a name or a proper burial. If a person agrees to carry a myling to a resting place, they will discover that the apparition grows heavier and heavier, until it is almost impossible to carry. If they drop the myling before fulfilling its needs, they risk dying as a result of its violent rage.

Once upon a time…
The Swedish word 'myling' means both 'a small murdered child' and 'a small child who murders', capturing the dual nature of this apparition.

Origins:
A myling is the vengeful ghost of a child who died or was murdered, and who was not given an official burial.

In popular culture:
In the 1960s, Astrid Lindgren wrote three novels about a mischievous boy called Emil of Lönneberge, who is told tales of mylings and other ghosts by the old lady Krösa-Maja.

Fylgia

he Old Norse word 'fylgia', meaning 'to accompany', describes an apparition that accompanies a person through life. Sometimes the fylgia can take the form of an animal, representing an aspect of its host's character, such as bravery, beauty or cunning. In other cases a fylgia may be a woman, an ancestral mother whose role is to protect her entire family or clan through the generations. Fylgjur (the plural form of fylgia) often appear during sleep, and they can cause nightmares if they choose to visit someone who is not their usual living partner. In Icelandic, the word 'fylgia' is also a word for the placenta, suggesting an origin for the idea of a person having a separate but attached part that is key to their identity.

Once upon a time...
In Irish folklore, the 'fetch' is a similar type of spirit, appearing in the form of a living person and often portending that person's death.

Origins:
In Norse legend, a fylgia is a spirit that accompanies a person and may signal information about their future fate.

In popular culture:
Although the fylgia does not appear in many modern films or television shows, there are several online quizzes where you can find your own fylgia to fit your personality.

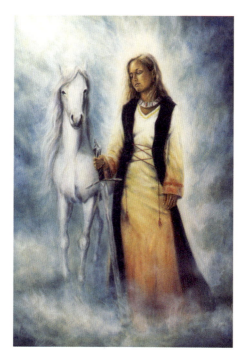

According to Norse tradition, fylgjur are spiritual companions who protect the living.

"Fear not death, for the hour of your doom is set, and no one can escape it."

– Saga of the Volsungs

"Consult the Genius of the Place in all."

– Alexander Pope, 'Epistles to Several Persons: Epistle IV'

Roman homes often contained an altar to their genius loci or 'spirit of the place'.

Genius loci

 n the altars of classical Roman temples, and in shrines in family homes, it was common to see a sculpture of a human figure holding an offering bowl, a snake or a cornucopia. Each of these figures was a genius loci, the protective spirit of a specific place. According to the Roman philosopher Seneca, the atmosphere created by a genius loci need not only be beautiful; it could also be eerie and overwhelming. In modern times, the habit of referring to a country, city or vessel as a person suggests that the concept of the genius loci is alive and well. In fact, the more we see our surroundings as having their own life, the more we might be willing to protect them in the face of environmental change.

Once upon a time…
In recent centuries, the principle of the genius loci has informed the development of architecture and landscape design.

Origins:
A genius loci is literally the 'spirit of a place', often playing a protective or guardianlike role.

In popular culture:
Fantasy novels and films often invoke the concept of a planet or spaceship that is sentient and acts on the urgings of its own genius loci.

Shades

According to ancient Greek beliefs, the moment of death saw a separation of soul and body: while the body decayed, the soul would continue to exist in a shadow-realm. Most souls would cross the River Styx to spend a bleak eternity in the Kingdom of Hades. Only the most extraordinary heroes would have the chance to enjoy the delights of Elysium, while punishment after death was reserved for the few greatest wrongdoers. Hades, the ruler of the Greek underworld, focused his attention on making sure that none of the shades of dwelled in his realm ever escaped back into the land of the living.

Once upon a time…
The concept of a shadow-realm is shared by many beliefs and traditions, particularly those of the ancient Near East.

Origins:
In Greek and Roman mythology, a shade is the spirit of a dead person who dwells in the underworld.

In popular culture:
The story of Orpheus's quest to rescue Eurydice from an eternity as a shade in Hades has been told from antiquity to the present day, including the 2024 Netflix series *Kaos*.

Shades are spirits that dwell in the underworld in eternal shadow.

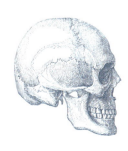

"Death submits to no one — so mortals hate him most of all the gods."

– *Homer,* Iliad

Vrykolakas

In Ancient Greece there was a belief that people who died could return to our world under certain circumstances, in an undead form, neither fully dead nor alive. A person who had led a sinful life, been buried in unconsecrated ground or eaten meat from an animal that had been attacked by a werewolf was at risk of returning as a vrykolakas, an animal with a swollen, drum-shaped body and a penchant for eating human flesh. To prevent loved ones returning in this terrifying form, people would resort to apotropaics: techniques designed to keep the dead in the grave where they belonged, such as burying the person upside-down or including a scythe or sickle in the grave with the body.

Once upon a time…
The roots of the word 'vrykolakas' can be traced to 'wolf' and 'strand of hair', meaning 'werewolf', although the Greek vrykolakas is more like a vampire.

Origins:
A vrykolakas is a zombie-like creature from Greek folklore who eats human flesh.

In popular culture:
The Greek island of Santorini is now famed for its beauty, but it was once feared as the home of a vast number of vrykolakas.

In Ancient Greece, it was believed that an unquiet soul could return to haunt the living as a Vrykolakas.

"When people die of a contagious disease … and they bury them without a priest, without anything, they become vrykolakes."

– *Description by 'Antonios' in an article by D. Demetracopoulou Lee*

Historical Ghosts

It is perhaps not surprising, when we consider how many wars and feuds have raged over the centuries, that our historical sites are richly populated with ghosts. It seems that every castle has overseen a tragedy, due to love, greed or ambition, and the generations who would later occupy these spiritually affected spaces have often come face to face with the unquiet souls of residents from former times. Ghosts are not restricted to palaces and fortresses; they can be found in theatres, hotels, political spaces and even ordinary homes, as we discover in this chapter. And maybe even your home has its own resident spectre…

Charles Macklin, who murdered another actor in the Theatre Royal in London, is just one of the historical ghosts haunting this chapter.

Agnes Sampson

ea journeys are often perilous, and not only to those who travel by ship. In 1590, a ship carrying King James VI of Scotland and his 14-year-old bride, Anne of Denmark, was caught in storms and had to seek shelter in Oslo, Norway. Rather than blame the weather for the dangerous voyage, King James settled on witchcraft as the source of the disturbance. A Scottish healer named Agnes Sampson was accused of being a witch, and after hours of appalling torture, she confessed to having caused the storm. After a trial, Agnes was garrotted and burned at the stake, and her ghost has been said to roam the Palace of Holyroodhouse in Edinburgh ever since.

Once upon a time…
In 2022, the first minister of Scotland issued a formal apology for the historical persecution of alleged witches in Scotland.

Origins:
Agnes was just one of over 100 people accused in the North Berwick Witch Trials, which were part of a wider European campaign with an estimated 100,000 victims.

In popular culture:
Agnes's story was investigated by historian Lucy Worsley in 2022 in a BBC documentary series.

Agnes Sampson and other so-called North Berwick Witches were tried before King James in 1591.

"His Maiestie had neuer come safelye from the Sea, if his faith had not prevailed above their ententions."

– *Quotation from Agnes Sampson's forced confession, 1591*

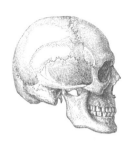

"A shout – and the cap was off and the flashbulb fired, with the results which we now see."

– Harry Price

Does this mysterious photograph truly show the ghost of The Brown Lady, or was it an act of camera trickery?

The Brown Lady

In 1936, *Country Life* magazine published a photograph that finally provided proof to any doubters of the existence of ghosts – or was it an elaborate hoax? The image, taken by Captain Hubert Provand and Indre Shira, shows the grand wooden staircase at Raynham Hall, with a transparent female figure in a long robe seemingly descending towards them. The ghost, known as the Brown Lady, was first seen by a guest in 1835, and then by Charles Dickens's friend Captain Frederick Marryat the following year. She is thought to be the spirit of Dorothy Walpole, who died in mysterious circumstances at the Hall in 1726, after an unhappy marriage to Charles Townshend, 2nd Viscount Townshend, the owner at the time.

Once upon a time...
According to the Norfolk Record Office, Dorothy Walpole's death was the result of smallpox, and not a more nefarious cause.

Origins:
The Brown Lady is a ghost who haunts Raynham Hall in Norfolk, and who was once apparently captured in a photographic image.

In popular culture:
Those who wish to explore the ghostly energies of Raynham Hall are able to book a glamping holiday in the grounds, in a luxury yurt that may or may not be haunted.

Banff Springs Hotel ghosts

In hotels, there are ever-changing and transient populations, which makes them hotspots for wandering spirits; when someone dies away from home, it's only natural that their ghost may not rest quietly. Canada's Banff Springs Hotel has been welcoming guests since the late nineteenth century, and some of them have overstayed their original bookings as unofficial ghostly residents. The most famous is the Ghost Bride, who died while descending a marble staircase in the hotel in the 1920s, and who is now sometimes seen gliding up and down those same stairs in her bridal veil. Other ghosts of the hotel include a helpful bellhop and an unseen figure who snatches pillows from under guest's heads as they sleep.

Once upon a time…
The Banff Springs Hotel was built in 1888 in Alberta, Canada, and is known as the 'Castle in the Rockies'.

Origins:
The earliest known haunting at the hotel dates back to the 1920s, with the appearance of the Ghost Bride.

In popular culture:
Visitors to the hotel can take a guided ghost tour, with a chance of meeting some of its famous spectral residents.

The Banff Spring Hotel in Canada's Rocky Mountains is home to more than one ghostly guest.

"Millions of spiritual creatures walk the earth Unseen, both when we wake, and when we sleep."

– *John Milton,* Paradise Lost

Scratching Fanny

eath, debt, slander and conspiracy: the case of Cock Lane entranced the public. In 1760, William Kent set up a home in London's Cock Lane with his late wife's sister, Frances Lyne, being unable to marry her under canon law. His landlord Richard Parsons lived in the same building with his daughter Elizabeth. When Frances, or Fanny, died of smallpox, Elizabeth claimed to hear knocking and scratching, and a story grew that these came from the deceased Fanny, lamenting her murder by Kent. An investigation meant the case ended up in court. The noises came from a piece of wood held by Elizabeth, and Kent was eventually pilloried for his crimes.

Once upon a time...
Cock Lane is a short street in London, close to Smithfield Market, St Bartholomew's Hospital and the Central Criminal Court.

Origins:
Scratching Fanny was the name given to a ghost who knocked on wood to show her presence, although she was deemed in court to have been a malicious hoax.

In popular culture:
Charles Dickens had a fascination for ghosts, and referred to the Cock Lane ghost in three of his novels: *Nicholas Nickleby*, *A Tale of Two Cities* and *Dombey and Son*.

The ghost of Cock Lane made her presence known by knocking on wood, to the bafflement of onlookers.

"*I forget … whether it was my great-grandfather who went to school with the Cock-lane Ghost, or the Thirsty Woman of Tutbury who went to school with my grandmother.*"

– *Charles Dickens*, Nicholas Nickleby

75

"We slept well all Night, but early before day in the Morning, I was awakened ... by a great knocking just without our Chamber door."

– *Joseph Glanvill*, Saducismus Triumphatus

When a judge confiscated The Drummer of Tedworth's instrument, the drumming noises moved into his own house.

The Drummer of Tedworth

ome street musicians are more welcome than others, and in 1661 in the town of Tedworth (now called Tidworth) in Wiltshire, a man called William Drury was busy annoying the townsfolk by playing his drum incessantly and begging for money. The local judge, John Mompesson, took Drury to court for having a counterfeit busking licence, and Drury's drum was confiscated and sent to Mompesson's house. The judge and his family began to hear ferocious banging all over the house, which lasted for two years and became so intense that the children were even shaken out of their beds. The case was debated far and wide, and deemed by many to be the result of a prank by the children, but only the Drummer himself knows for certain.

Once upon a time…
This story of the Drummer of Tedworth was the first recorded report of a poltergeist in Britain.

Origins:
The Drummer of Tedworth is a poltergeist whose actions were observed in Wiltshire in the 1660s.

In popular culture:
Joseph Addison wrote a play called *The Drummer*, based on the events in Tedworth, in 1716, with the setting updated to the War of the Spanish Succession.

The Ghost Nun of Borley Rectory

In the Essex village of Borley there once stood an elegant Victorian rectory, built in 1862 for the local vicar, Henry Dawson Ellis Bull, and later extended to accommodate his family of 14 children. As the years passed, a number of supernatural phenomena were observed, including unexplained footsteps and even two headless horseman driving a ghostly carriage. In 1900, the spectral figure of a nun was seen by four of the vicar's daughters, and in 1938, this same nun made contact during a séance and gave her name as Marie Lairre. In 1939, when the rectory was damaged in a fire, a local woman said she saw the nun's ghostly face in an upstairs window as the flames raged.

Once upon a time…
The psychic researcher Harry Price lived in Borley Rectory for a year and described it as 'the most haunted house in England'.

Origins:
The ghost of Borley Rectory was believed to be the spirit of a nun from a nearby Benedictine monastery who had an affair with a monk.

In popular culture:
Borley Rectory has frequently been featured on film and television, from a BBC investigation in 1975 to two films directed by Steven M. Smith in 2019 and 2021.

Borley Rectory in Essex was once known as 'the most haunted house in England'.

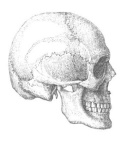

"… A glass candlestick was hurled at me, the bells rang, and I saw keys fall from keyholes for no apparent reason."

– Harry Price, 'The Most Haunted House in England'

"Whether there ever was any such sect [as Voodoo], and whether Marie was ever its queen, her life was one to render such a belief possible."

– The New York Times *obituary of Marie Laveau, 23 June 1881*

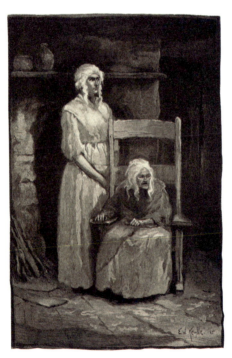

Marie Laveau lived an extraordinary life, and continued to make a ghostly impression long after her death.

Marie Laveau, the Voodoo Queen

Marie Laveau was born in the French Quarter of New Orleans in 1801 as a free woman of colour. She lived a vividly full life, tending to the sick and caring for prisoners who had been sentenced to death, often interceding for them and sometimes succeeding in averting their executions. Laveau was also an active practitioner of Voodoo, helping people deal with disputes, financial difficulties and health problems, and she rose to the rank of Voodoo Queen in the mid-19th century. When she died in 1881, she was buried in Saint Louis Cemetery No. 1, and her ghost has been seen many times ever since, both in the cemetery and in locations across the French Quarter.

Once upon a time…
Louisiana Voodoo arose from a combination of the practices of Roman Catholicism, Haitian Vodou and West African traditional religions.

Origins:
Marie Laveau (1801–1881) was a practitioner of Voodoo in New Orleans, Louisiana, and also a midwife and herbalist.

In popular culture:
Marie Laveau has inspired countless songs and novels, and even a stage musical, called *Marie Christine*, which is based on the events of her life and premiered in 1999.

The Ghosts of the Dakota, New York

It is not surprising that New York is a city abundantly populated with ghosts, and the location that offers the most is the Dakota, a cooperative apartment building overlooking Central Park. One of the supernatural inhabitants is a little girl with blonde hair, who is often seen bouncing a red rubber ball. Another is a boy of approximately 10 years old, who appeared in 1965, wearing a suit in the style of 1900. Down in the building's basement, the activities of a poltergeist have been all too evident, with tools and rubbish being thrown around and nearly injuring people. It is thought that the spectre causing all the trouble was the building's first owner, Edward Cabot Clark, who did not live to see its completion.

Once upon a time…
The Dakota was named as a reference to its distance from what was in 1880 the fashionable heart of New York – as far away, metaphorically, as the Dakota territory.

Origins:
The Dakota is an apartment building in New York designed in the German Renaissance style. It was constructed between 1880 and 1884.

In popular culture:
On 8 December 1980, the musician John Lennon was shot and fatally wounded outside the Dakota, where he lived, by Mark David Chapman.

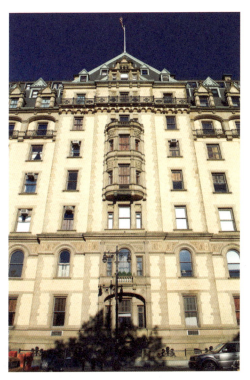

New York's elegant Dakota building is home to a diverse population of supernatural residents.

"Maybe all the people who say ghosts don't exist are just afraid to admit that they do."

– *Michael Ende,* The Neverending Story

"Goddamn you for a blackguard, scrub, rascal!"

– Words spoken by Charles Macklin as he murdered Thomas Hallam in 1735

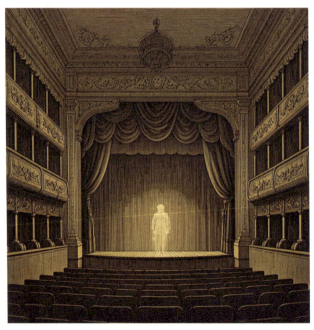

A man in eighteenth-century costume is just one of the characters you may encounter at the Theatre Royal in London.

The Man in Grey, Theatre Royal

ne afternoon in London's Theatre Royal on Drury Lane, you might be sitting peacefully in the upper circle only to be surprised by the passing sight of a young man dressed in a grey suit in the fashion of the 18th century, with powdered hair and a three-pointed hat. If so, your eyes have alighted on the famous Man in Grey, the best-known of the theatre's cast of spectral residents. No one knows why he continues to appear or who caused his death, but he is a firm part of the theatre's spiritual scenery. Other regular hauntings are the clown Joseph Grimaldi, and the Irish actor Charles Macklin, who killed fellow actor Thomas Hallam in the theatre in 1735.

Once upon a time…
The current Theatre Royal, which opened in 1812, is the fourth theatre to have stood on the same site, making it London's oldest continuous theatrical site.

Origins:
The Man in Grey is just one of many ghosts to have been seen in the Theatre Royal.

In popular culture:
It is thought that the Man in Grey only attends performances of successful shows, meaning that his appearances are welcomed by the actors who see him.

Marie Antoinette

t took place on a hot August day in 1901, two Englishwomen, Charlotte Anne Moberly and Eleanor Jourdain, were strolling in the gardens of the Palace of Versailles in search of the Petit Trianon, a chateau that had once been the home of Marie Antoinette, the wife of King Louis XVI. Losing their way, they passed people wearing odd historical costumes, with three-cornered hats and long coats. As they continued, they both felt an oppressive atmosphere and Moberly saw an elegant woman in an old-fashioned gown, sitting sketching on a lawn. Afterwards, Moberly and Jourdain agreed they had experienced a supernatural encounter – and that the artist was almost certainly the late Queen of France.

Once upon a time...
Marie Antoinette was Queen of France from 1774 until her execution on 16 October 1793 during the French Revolution.

Origins:
The Petit Trianon is a small chateau in the grounds of the vast Palace of Versailles in France.

In popular culture:
Moberly and Jourdain's book *An Adventure* was very popular, going through six editions between 1911 and 1955.

Marie Antoinette's ghost remained in the gardens of the Palace of Versailles long after her death in 1793.

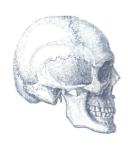

"*… On a certain day in August Marie Antoinette is regularly seen at the Petit Trianon, with a light flapping hat and a pink dress.*"

– *Eleanor Jourdain writing as Frances Lamont,* An Adventure

"I heard the sound of a taffeta dress moving/rustling, and without wishing to sound dramatic, definitely felt a presence."

– David Heaton, former facilities manager at No. 10 Downing Street

While London's 10 Downing Street has seen many prime ministers pass through, its ghosts recognise no elections.

The Ghosts of 10 Downing St

While No. 10 Downing Street may well be haunted by the ghosts of policies that were never enacted, it is also inhabited by a motley band of spirits. Ghost sightings include a man in a top hat who walks through doors, a little girl who holds the hands of people visiting the basement, and the unexplained scent of Winston Churchill's cigar smoke. In the early years of the 21st century, No. 10 facilities manager David Heaton was preparing the dining room for an event when he felt another presence in the room, wearing a rustling dress. He then discovered that this ghost had also been seen by colleagues: a lady in a white ballgown who passes through the staterooms.

Once upon a time…
George Downing, after whom Downing Street is named, was a preacher who became a member of parliament, an ambassador and a spymaster for Oliver Cromwell.

Origins:
No. 10 Downing Street has been the residence of many prime ministers of the United Kingdom since 1732.

In popular culture:
In autumn 2022, Liz Truss became the UK's shortest-serving prime minister. Her 49-day period in office was haunted by the live-stream of a lettuce, with bets placed on which would survive longer.

Annie Morgan

n the late 19th century, spiritualism was popular with the public and a topic for serious research by scientists of the day. Mediums hosted séances where interested parties could connect with voices from the spirit world, and sometimes even meet these long-deceased people in the flesh. Annie Owen Morgan, said to be the daughter of the 17th-century pirate Henry Morgan, was one of these talkative spirits, who also appeared as Katie King. The medium who received Annie's messages was a London teenager, Florence Cook, who amazed audiences by seemingly causing Annie and Katie to appear in person in her rooms, although sceptics reported Florence was never to be found during these appearances.

Once upon a time…
Sir William Crookes, who supported Florence Cook's claims to be in contact with the spirit world, was also a scientist, and discovered the element thallium.

Origins:
Annie Morgan, also known as Katie King, was a spirit who communicated through the Victorian medium Florence Cook.

In popular culture:
illustrated engraving from the 1870s shows the spirit of Katie King – also known as Annie Morgan – appearing at a séance in Philadelphia.

Annie Morgan, a seventeenth-century young woman, returned as a spirit in séances some 200 years later.

"From Annie Owen de Morgan (alias 'Katie') to her friend, Florence Marryat Ross-Church. With love. Pensez a moi. — May 21st, 1874."

– Note written by the 'spirit' Kate King, according to Florence Marryat

Nan Tuck's Ghost

uxted today is a peaceful village in East Sussex, but its history is not without drama. According to local legend, there was once a woman called Nan Tuck, who lived in the nearby village of Rotherfield. When Nan's husband died, her neighbours suspected something was amiss, and concluded that she had poisoned him. Nan decided to flee the village, and sought sanctuary in Buxted's parish church, but she wasn't fast enough to evade her pursuers. Fearing for her life, she ran into the woods – and disappeared. Although Nan was never captured, her ghost has been seen several times over the years by travellers on the road now known as Nan Tuck's Lane.

Once upon a time…
The entire village of Buxted, apart from its church, was relocated in the 1830s so that the owner of the local manor house could extend his parkland.

Origins:
Nan Tuck is said to have poisoned her husband to death and then vanished in the woods while fleeing.

In popular culture:
The legend of Nan Tuck has inspired poetry and still draws visitors to Buxted Woods in search of her ghost.

Nan Tuck's unquiet spirit still haunts the Sussex woodland where she fled from justice.

*"With gentle hand
Touch – for there is a spirit
in the woods."*

– William Wordsworth, 'Nutting'

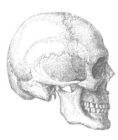

*"In shuddering amazement
his hearers all stared,
Whilst, with half-lessened terror,
Falconis declared
He had met with a murder'd man's Sprite."*

– Felix, 'The Sprite of the Creek'

*Dave Rigelsford and Gordon Thomas sitting where Fisher's
ghost solved his own murder over a century before, 1948.*

Fisher's Ghost

ampbelltown in New South Wales is now a bustling satellite city of Sydney, but back in the early 19th century it was a remote rural outpost, and the perfect place for an Englishman, Frederick Fisher, to build a new life as a farmer. When Fisher suddenly disappeared in 1826, his neighbour George Worrall explained that he had decided to return to England – and coincidentally, had generously given Worrall his farm. Not long afterwards, another farmer saw Fisher's ghost sitting on a bridge over the creek, pointing mournfully to a nearby field. When police dug up the site under the guidance of an Aboriginal tracker named Namut, Fisher's body was discovered, and Worrall was hanged for his murder.

Once upon a time…
Both Frederick Fisher and his murderer George Worrall had been transported as convicts to Australia from England, before obtaining Tickets of Leave that allowed them to purchase property as free men.

Origins:
The tale of Fisher's ghost is a well-known folk legend in Australia, originating in the early nineteenth century.

In popular culture:
Campbelltown hosts a Festival of Fisher's Ghost every year to celebrate the creative energy, spirit and pride of the local community.

Napoleon

n history he is one of the most famous leaders of all time, Napoleon led his troops to many victories but his defeat at Waterloo in 1815 saw the end of his military career. Shortly afterwards he was exiled to St Helena, an island in the Atlantic Ocean over a thousand miles from the nearest major landmass. When his body was disinterred in 1840, a soldier of the 91st Argyllshire Highlanders reported hearing a terrible noise, which all agreed must be Napoleon trying to break out of his coffin. They planned to scare the ghost into submission by speaking in made-up Russian, but the soldier chosen for the task was knocked over by a goat before he could begin.

Once upon a time…
Napoleon Bonaparte was born in Corsica in 1769 and died in exile on the island of St Helena on 5 May 1821.

Origins:
In 1840, Napoleon's body was taken to France and given a state funeral, before being buried at Les Invalides, Paris.

In popular culture:
Charlotte Brontë, aged 17, wrote a humorous story called 'Napoleon and the Spectre', in which Napoleon receives a ghostly visitor.

*On disturbing Napoleon's grave to move his body back to France,
British soldiers heard him shouting from within his coffin.*

*"We are born, we live, and we die
in the midst of the marvellous."*

– *Napoleon Bonaparte*

"Spookiness is the real purpose of the ghost story. It should give you the creeps and disturb your thoughts…"

— *Roald Dahl,* Roald Dahl's Book of Ghost Stories

Built in 1885, Monte Cristo Homestead retains its bygone elegance, and its ghostly apparitions, to this day.

Monte Cristo Homestead

In the later years of the 19th century, Christopher William Crawley and his wife Elizabeth spotted an opportunity and established a hotel for travellers on the railway line at Junee in New South Wales. Their hard work paid off, and in 1885 they built a commanding home overlooking Junee: the Monte Cristo Homestead. After the last Crawley left the house in 1948, it stood empty until it was brought back to life by the Ryan family. The Ryans noticed strange phenomena in the house: lights would switch on and off, pets would refuse to enter, and ghostly figures of a young boy, a woman and the late Christopher Crawley were seen. No wonder Monte Cristo is known as Australia's most haunted house.

Once upon a time…
The Monte Cristo Homestead is an elegant Victorian manor house that was built in 1885 in the town of Junee, New South Wales, Australia.

Origins:
After the house fell into disrepair, it was bought by the Ryan family in the 1960s and opened as a museum in the 1980s.

In popular culture:
The house is now open for visitors to explore, and a documentary about the Monte Cristo Homestead is currently in production.

Resurrection Mary

icture the scene: you are driving through the city at night and you pick up a lone female hitchhiker. She asks you to take her to the nearby cemetery, but when you get there, she disappears right next to you. This is precisely the experience recounted by several people in Chicago from the 1930s to the present day. According to local accounts, Mary was a young woman with blue eyes and blonde hair who went out dancing at the Oh Henry Ballroom in Chicago, wearing a white dress. On her walk home, she was struck and killed by a hit-and-run driver, and buried by her grieving parents in Resurrection Cemetery. But while her body may lie at rest, her soul has clearly not yet found peace.

Once upon a time…
The Chicago ballroom where Mary danced on the night of her death was named after a popular chocolate bar, the Oh Henry!

Origins:
Resurrection Mary is thought to be the ghost of a young woman who was hit by a car and now hitchhikes to Resurrection Cemetery in Chicago.

In popular culture:
The legend of Resurrection Mary has been featured on *Arthur C. Clarke's World of Strange Powers* and *Unsolved Mysteries*, and films named after her were released in 2006 and 2007.

The ghost of Resurrection Mary has been seen several times by drivers in Chicago ever since the 1930s.

"And that's when it happened. I looked to my left ... And when I turned she was gone. Vanished!"

– *Eyewitness account in an article by Bill Geist in* The Suburban Trib

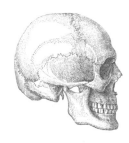

"When thoroughly reliable people encounter ghosts, their stories are difficult to explain away."

– *C.B. Colby,* Strangely Enough

Jack Sturgus, the Anchorage Chief of Police, was gunned down in 1921 in an alley behind the Anchorage Hotel.

The Ghosts of Anchorage Hotel

he original Anchorage Hotel was established in 1916, and for many years was the primary meeting place in the new territory of Alaska. Today's Historic Anchorage Hotel stands on the site of the first hotel's annex, and is particularly popular with guests seeking a ghostly encounter. Back in 1921, Jack Sturges, Anchorage's first chief of police, was shot in the back just outside today's hotel, and his killer was never found. He is said to revisit the scene of his death every year, trying to close his own very cold case. The ghost of a young girl has been seen on the second floor of the hotel, and staff and guests alike have watched in shock as picture frames and mirrors launch themselves from walls.

Once upon a time…
Anchorage was first established as a tent city in 1915 in an area that has been inhabited seasonally by Alaska Natives since 3000–4000 BCE.

Origins:
Staff and guests at Alaska's Historic Anchorage Hotel have seen numerous apparitions and heard unexplained sounds and voices.

In popular culture:
After-dark ghost tours of Anchorage allow visitors to explore the Historic Anchorage Hotel, the Hotel Captain Cook and the Boney Courthouse.

Queen Esther

he Battle of Wyoming, which took place on 3 July 1778, is also known as the Wyoming Massacre to mark the fact that some 300 people on the Patriot side were killed by a combined force of Loyalist and Iroquois fighters. One of the Iroquois leaders was a woman called Queen Esther, who may have been motivated to lead the attack after her son had been killed in a drunken argument just days earlier. According to one account, Queen Esther was hanged, after watching the execution of all the women and children of her community. Her weeping ghost has reportedly been seen hanging from the tree where she died.

Once upon a time…
The American Revolutionary War of 1775–1783 saw over 200 battles and skirmishes and caused hundreds of thousands of deaths, as Americans fought to free themselves from British rule.

Origins:
Esther Montour, known as Queen Esther, was an Iroquois Native American woman who lived in the eighteenth century.

In popular culture:
'Queen Esther's Rock' in Wyoming, Pennsylvania has a sign saying 'a vengeful Indian woman' murdered 14 captive American soldiers here on 3 July 1778.

Iroquois Queen Esther was hanged after the Battle of Wyoming in 1778, and her weeping ghost was seen after her death.

"Sweet Wyoming! the day when thou art doom'd, Guiltless, to mourn thy loveliest bowers laid low!"

– *Thomas Campbell, 'Gertrude of Wyoming'*

105

The Ghosts of the Battle of Gettysburg

he three-day-long Battle of Gettysburg of 1863 marked a turning point of the American Civil War, although it would be two long years more before the Confederacy was finally defeated. It is perhaps not surprising that such an extended and bloody battle would leave ghostly traces behind for future generations to discover. On the battlefield, a hill called the Devil's Den is still haunted by fallen soldiers, and at Little Round Top, actors in the 1993 film *Gettysburg* were joined by a Union soldier who handed them original 19th-century musket rounds and then left. Beyond the battlegrounds, the Herr Tavern became the first hospital for Confederate soldiers, and is now haunted by spectres of men who died there.

Once upon a time…
The American Civil War was a conflict between the Union and the Confederacy, and lasted from 1861 to 1865.

Origins:
The Battle of Gettysburg of 1–3 July 1863 was the bloodiest battle of the American Civil War, causing over 50,000 casualties across both sides.

In popular culture:
Nearly one million people visit the battlefield at Gettysburg every year, to explore both its military history and its supernatural legacy.

Ghosts of the soldiers who died at the Battle of Gettysburg in 1863 have been seen roaming the battlefield.

"The brave men, living and dead, who struggled here have consecrated [this ground], far above our poor power to add or detract."

– Abraham Lincoln, *Gettysburg Address*

"And thus I take my leave of the world and of you all, and I heartily desire you all to pray for me."

– *Anne Boleyn's final speech*

Anne Boleyn was executed at the command of her husband Henry VIII in 1533 at the Tower of London.

Anne Boleyn

ing Henry VIII made history when he married Anne Boleyn at Westminster Abbey in 1533. His first wife, Catherine of Aragon, was still living, and his decision to divorce her in favour of Anne caused an irreparable rift between the monarchy and the Catholic church. At first all went well, but by 1536, when Anne had failed to provide Henry with a son, fortune turned against her, and she was convicted of adultery, incest and treason, and sentenced to death in the Tower of London. Her ghost has been seen in the Tower many times; on one dramatic occasion, a guard saw a procession of noblemen and women in the Chapel Royal, with Queen Anne at their head.

Once upon a time…
Anne's ghost has been seen in numerous other locations, including Hever Castle, Blickling Hall, where she was born, and Marwell Hall.

Origins:
Anne Boleyn was the second wife of King Henry VIII, who had her executed in 1536. Her daughter grew up to become Queen Elizabeth I.

In popular culture:
Anne's story has been retold on the page, stage and screen for centuries, from Donizetti's 1830 opera *Anna Bolena* to the hit musical *Six*.

The Grey Lady, Bolsover Castle

he fortunes of Bolsover Castle in Derbyshire have waxed and waned over the centuries since its founding in Norman England. It has fallen into ruin more than once, only to rise up in a new and grander form each time. Such a turbulent history must inevitably be connected with supernatural occurrences. The most famous of the castle's ghosts is a nameless Grey Lady, who has been seen on multiple occasions by visitors and staff. One theory says she is endlessly searching for her lost child, while another suggests that she was a bride-to-be whose groom died in a tragic accident before they could be married.

Once upon a time…
Bolsover Castle was founded by the Peverel family in the 12th century and rebuilt into its current form in the 17th century.

Origins:
The Grey Lady is just one of the ghosts of Bolsover Castle, along with a cavalier on horseback, a small boy and a woman in black.

In popular culture:
In 2017, staff of English Heritage voted Bolsover No. 1 of its top spookiest properties, many of them having experienced ghostly goings-on there.

The Grey Lady of Bolsover Castle in Derbyshire has often been observed by staff and visitors.

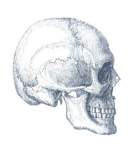

"On a dark night, the ghosts emerge to fright."

— *Anonymous saying about Bolsover Castle*

111

The Green Lady, Château de Brissac

In a tragic tale of jealousy and forbidden love the haunting of the imposing Château de Brissac in Angers, France began. Jacques de Brezé (c.1440–1494) married Charlotte, an illegitimate daughter of King Charles VII of France. Theirs was not a politically expedient match, and Charlotte fell in love with Jacques' friend Pierre de Lavergne. When Jacques caught the lovers, he killed them both, and although he escaped with only a fine, the building has been haunted ever since by Charlotte's unquiet spirit. Visitors have seen Charlotte's ghost wandering in the château wearing a green dress. Those who see her never forget it, where her eyes and nose should be, there are only gaping holes.

Once upon a time…
The original Château de Brissac was built in the 11th century by the counts of Anjou and was rebuilt in 1611 to become the tallest château in France.

Origins:
The Green Lady is a ghost thought to be Charlotte de Brezé, who was murdered by her jealous husband in 1477.

In popular culture:
The château is now open for visitor tours, and it is also possible to book an overnight stay – though sightings of the Green Lady are sadly not guaranteed.

Slain by her jealous husband, the ghost of the Green Lady haunts the Château de Brissac in France.

*"Of joys departed,
Not to return, how painful the remembrance!"*

– *Robert Blair,* The Grave

"The spirit-world around this world of sense
Floats like an atmosphere, and everywhere
Wafts through these earthly mists
and vapours dense
A vital breath of more ethereal air."

– *Henry Wadsworth Longfellow*

Chillingham Castle in Northumberland is an ideal place
to go on a ghost hunt.

The Blue Boy, Chillingham Castle

orthumberland's Chillingham Castle is famed for its ghosts, one of whom was a boy dressed in a blue suit in the style of the 1660s. Nobody knew his origin, but one day in the 1920s, workmen discovered the bones of a child buried in a wall near the site of the hauntings, along with scraps of blue clothing. The child's remains were buried in a nearby churchyard, and the hauntings seemed to stop, but to this day people report seeing blue balls of light in the castle's windows at night. The Blue Boy is not the only spectre in the castle. Visitors have seen a grey lady, thought to be Lady Mary Berkeley, who died in 1719, and a woman in white, who appears in the pantry begging for a drink of water.

Once upon a time…
Chillingham Castle in Northumberland was built as a medieval monastery, and later became a key stronghold on the border between England and Scotland.

Origins:
The Blue Boy is the ghost of an unknown child whose body was discovered in a wall of Chillingham Castle in the 1920s.

In popular culture:
Chillingham is marketed today as 'Britain's most haunted historic castle', offering regular ghost tours and ghost hunts to brave visitors.

Alice and Felix, Château de Fougeret

ould you spend the night in a haunted castle? Travellers in France's New Aquitaine region are invited to do just that, at the Château de Fougeret. Built in the 14th century, this castle was purchased by Veronique and François-Joseph Geffroy in 2009, and from the moment they arrived, they noticed uncanny goings-on such as vanishing objects, mysterious echoes and unseen voices. Among the castle's many ghosts are Felix, a broken-hearted man who took his life in 1898, and Alice, who died only four months after marrying the Viscount of France in 1924. Alice's ghost manifests as a scent of incense in her bedroom, while Felix makes his presence felt by moving objects in his office.

Once upon a time…
The castle's history has been beset by disputes over succession, with a tragedy affecting every generation that lived there.

Origins:
The château is believed to have been constructed on an ancient druidic site, where local villagers would come to find a cure for their ills.

In popular culture:
The Château de Fougeret has frequently been featured on television as a ghost-filled site, and online videos about it have attracted millions of views.

The Château de Fougeret in France has attracted researchers of the supernatural ever since its current owners arrived in 2009.

"I do not believe in ghosts, but I fear them."

– *Germaine de Staël*, Recollections of Past Life

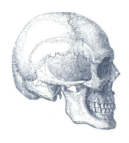

"How could I help writing romances when I had walked ... through that long gallery, ... mused in those tapestried chambers, and peeped, with bristling hair, into the shadowy abysses of Hell-hole?"

– *Edward Bulwer-Lytton*

Knebworth House in Hertfordshire is an atmospheric location in which to encounter ghostly spirits.

Spinning Jenny, Knebworth House

ny ancient home is likely to accrue spooky tales over the centuries, and Hertfordshire's Knebworth House is no exception. One of its resident apparitions is Spinning Jenny, said to be the spirit of a young woman who was shut away with her spinning wheel to keep her from meeting an unsuitable lover. Another ghostly inhabitant is a young boy who glows with a radiant light. The author Sir Walter Scott described being told by Lord Castlereagh that he had seen a glowing boy emerge from the embers of a dying fire in a bedroom, walk towards him, and then gradually diminish. Following Castlereagh's suicide in 1822, any sighting of this ghostly boy was feared to be an omen of untimely death.

Once upon a time…
Knebworth House in Hertfordshire has been home to the Lytton family since 1490, and also hosts a well-known summer music festival in its grounds.

Origins:
Spinning Jenny and the Yellow Boy are two ghosts whose origin is not known, that have been seen at Knebworth House.

In popular culture:
In the autumn of 2024, Charli XCX and Emma Corrin reportedly felt aware of ghostly presences during the filming of *100 Nights of Hero* at Knebworth House.

The Grey Lady, Glamis Castle

To be the enemy of a king is a most unfortunate circumstance, and it is one that Janet Douglas, Lady Glamis, ended up in through no fault of her own. Her brother had imprisoned the teenage King James V of Scotland under his period of guardianship, from 1528; when James escaped, the entire family was disgraced. In 1537 Janet was accused of planning to poison the king. The evidence needed to convict her was obtained through the torture of her servants and family members, and she was burned at the stake on Castle Hill in Edinburgh in front of her 16-year-old son. Her ghost is now seen, dressed in grey, roaming through the Clock Tower and chapel of Glamis Castle.

Once upon a time...
King James V's hatred for Janet's family ran deep, as her brother, the 6th Earl of Angus, was his stepfather and had kept the young king imprisoned as a teenager.

Origins:
Janet Douglas, Lady Glamis, was executed by burning in 1537, having been found guilty of treason.

In popular culture:
Glamis Castle is famous as the fictional home of Macbeth in Shakespeare's play, and in real life it was the scene of King Malcolm II's murder in 1034.

Janet Douglas was burned at the stake on charges of witchcraft in 1537 in Edinburgh.

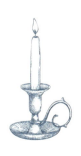

*"Black spirits and white,
Red spirits and grey,
Mingle, mingle, mingle,
You that mingle may."*

– *William Shakespeare*, Macbeth

*"By a temple and from a tomb
I send thee warning."*

– *Edward Bulwer-Lytton*, Pausanias, the Spartan

*Pausanias of Sparta haunted temple-goers until his spirit was released
by visiting necromancers.*

Pausanias of Sparta

ausanias, a great general and regent of Sparta, was hailed as a war hero after defeating the Persians at Plataea, but shortly afterwards he was accused of conspiring with his former enemies and betraying his own people. His punishment was to be walled up in the Temple of Athena and starved to death, with his own mother laying the first brick. After this torturous death, Pausanias's ghost appeared to temple visitors, and the Spartans asked the Oracle at Delphi how they could end this source of terror. On the Oracle's advice, they hired professional necromancers, who managed to free Pausanias's unquiet soul from the walls where he had died in such agony.

Once upon a time…
In 479 BC, Pausanias led the Greeks to a historic victory over the Persian army at the Battle of Plataea.

Origins:
Pausanias was suspected of conspiracy with Xerxes I, the Persian king who had defeated his uncle Leonidas I at Thermopylae in 480 BC.

In popular culture:
As well as appearing in classical texts by Thucydides and Diodorus, Pausanias is a character in the video game *Assassin's Creed: Odyssey*.

"He asked nothing but justice of Heaven, and of man he asked only a fair field."

– Chronicle of the Cid

After his death, El Cid continued to fill his enemies with fear, as his corpse was ridden out into the battlefield.

El Cid

Spain in the 11th century was turbulent, especially in Léon and Castile, where after the death of Ferdinand the Great in 1065, his sons waged war over their inheritances. The military commander El Cid served Ferdinand's son Sancho before being exiled by his brother Alfonso after Sancho's death. El Cid went on to fight for the Muslim rulers of Zaragoza, and then led his own troops to establish himself as the ruler of Valencia. He died as Valencia was being besieged by the Berber Almoravids, according to legend his widow Jimena ordered his body to be strapped to his horse and ridden into battle, to terrify their enemies into submission. The 'ghost' of El Cid then won a thundering charge against Valencia's attackers.

Once upon a time…
Rodrigo Díaz, who would grow up to become El Cid, was born in Vivar in the north of Spain in c.1043.

Origins:
The nickname El Cid is derived from the Spanish Arabic *al-sīd*, meaning 'the Lord'.

In popular culture:
The life of El Cid has inspired plays, operas, poetry and films, including the historical epic *El Cid* starring Charlton Heston in 1961.

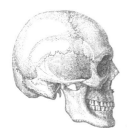

Ghosts from Literature

Ghosts have fascinated writers and artists throughout history, from the earliest tellers of tales to the novelists and film makers of today. Some are scary, and others friendly. Some seek vengeance, while others are happy to co-exist peacefully with the living. They can appear in a human form, or manifest as unsettling phenomena such as sounds and smells. On stage, on film and on the printed page, ghosts take many forms, revealing truths about the characters who see them and the artists who create them. Beware: this chapter is bewitched with spoilers, which may haunt your future reading and viewing experiences if you enter unprepared!

Literature is rich in ghosts, such as the spirits who haunt Ebenezer Scrooge in Dickens' A Christmas Carol.

Armida

iterary history overflows with stories of dangerous love across divides of nationality and religion, and Armida and Rinaldo's struggles rival those of Romeo and Juliet, even though they are less well known today than the teenage Veronese lovers. Armida, an enchantress, casts a spell on the crusader Rinaldo to make him fall in love with her, so that she can easily kill him. But before she can strike the fatal blow with her dagger, her own heart fills with feelings of love towards him, and she spares him. When Rinaldo is rescued by his fellow soldiers and the spell is broken, Armida, filled with rage, swears to pursue him as a ghost from the afterlife.

Once upon a time…
The characters of Armida and Rinaldo were created by Italian poet Torquato Tasso, in his epic poem *Gerusalemme Liberata (Jerusalem Delivered)*, published in 1581.

Origins:
Jean-Baptiste Lully's opera *Armide*, first performed in 1686, transforms Tasso's peaceful conclusion to Armida's story into one of rage and vengeance.

In popular culture:
The story has also inspired operas by several other composers, including Handel, Vivaldi, Haydn, Rossini, Dvořák and Weir.

*Love, jealousy and magic combine in the legend of Armida and Rinaldo,
as shown in this painting by Giovanni Battista Tiepolo.*

*"I will die if you leave, do not doubt it,
Ungrateful one, without you I cannot live.
But after my death, you will not avoid
My ghost relentlessly following you"*

– *English translation of Philippe Quinault's* Libretto *to Armide
by Jean-Baptiste Lully*

*"Murder most foul, as in the best it is,
But this most foul, strange,
and unnatural."*

– *William Shakespeare,* Hamlet, *Act 1, Scene 5*

*The ghost of Hamlet's father appears to him in Act I
of Shakespeare's famous tragedy.*

The Ghost of Hamlet's father

hakespeare's famous tragedy *Hamlet* opens not with the young Prince Hamlet but with Danish soldiers at Elsinore describing a ghost they have seen: a figure resembling the late king, whose name was also Hamlet, dressed in armour. The ghost is stubbornly silent until it meets Hamlet, who is troubled by the speed with which his uncle Claudius has taken the throne and married his mother Gertrude. Hamlet's late father explains how Claudius killed him as he slept, pouring a fatal poison into his ear, and calls on his son to avenge him, before departing with the heart-breaking words, 'Adieu, adieu, adieu. Remember me.' This first untimely death will be followed by many more before the final curtain falls.

Once upon a time…
Hamlet was written between 1599 and 1601. Shakespeare may have played the Ghost, though we will never know for sure.

Origins:
In Norse mythology, the death of Horvendill, king of the Jutes, was avenged by his son, Amleth.

In popular culture:
Hamlet's ghost has been portrayed on screen by Brian Blessed, John Gielgud, Paul Scofield, Sam Shepard and Patrick Stewart.

Banquo's Ghost

William Shakespeare's tragic play *Macbeth*, first performed in 1606, is famous for its three witches and the gradual descent into madness of the title character and his wife. It also includes one of the great theatrical ghosts in Banquo. At the start of the play, Banquo and Macbeth both receive cryptic prophecies from the witches, saying that Macbeth will become king, and Banquo the father of kings. When King Duncan is conveniently murdered, Banquo becomes suspicious of Macbeth, who arranges for him to be killed too. But his spirit returns to haunt Macbeth, and in the end, it is Banquo's son Fleance who inherits the throne.

Once upon a time...
Although an earlier version of the story made Banquo a conspirator in King Duncan's death, Shakespeare may have given him a more innocent character in order not to offend his descendant, King James I.

Origins:
The bloodied ghost of Banquo appears to Macbeth at a banquet, although nobody else in the room can see him.

In popular culture:
On stage and screen, Banquo's ghost has appeared as an actor, a green silhouette, a shaft of blue light, and as Macbeth's own shadow.

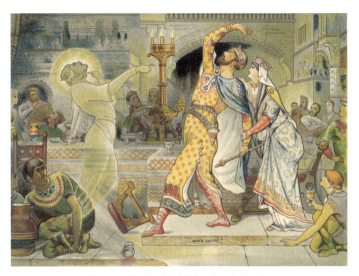

It's unsurprising that Macbeth loses his appetite when the ghost of Banquo appears at his table.

"Thou canst not say I did it.
Never shake
Thy gory locks at me."

– *William Shakespeare*, Macbeth

The Headless Horseman

n Washington Irving's famous short story, Ichabod Crane, a lanky, penniless schoolteacher dreams of marrying Katrina Van Tassel, set to inherit her father's wealth. However, the town jock Brom Bones also has his eyes on the beautiful heiress and hates competition. When Crane refuses to respond to provocation, Bones switches to a campaign of pranks to undermine him. One night, after being turned down by Katrina, Ichabod is riding through the woods when he meets a terrifying figure, the Galloping Hessian: a headless horseman who pursues him and then throws his head at the terrified teacher. When the head is in fact a pumpkin, we are forced to wonder whether the ghost was truly supernatural or not.

Once upon a time…
The idea of a headless horseman has roots in many northern European traditions, and usually signals misfortune for the person who encounters it.

Origins:
Washington Irving's short story was published in 1820 in a collection titled *The Sketch Book of Geoffrey Crayon, Gent.'*.

In popular culture:
Several films based on Irving's spooky tale have been made, including a Disney animation in 1949 and a Tim Burton production in 1999.

The Headless Horseman terrifies schoolmaster Ichabod Crane in Washington Irving's story 'The Legend of Sleepy Hollow'.

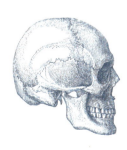

"…Gigantic in height, and muffled in a cloak, Ichabod was horror-struck on perceiving that he was headless!"

– *Washington Irving*, The Legend of Sleepy Hollow

"The weather was so stormy that the sailors said they saw the Flying Dutchman."

– *John MacDonald,* Travels in various part of Europe, Asia and Africa during a series of thirty years and upward

The Flying Dutchman, *shown here in a painting by Udo J. Keppler, was cursed to sail eternally.*

The Flying Dutchman

hen sailing on the high seas, it is all too easy to imagine disappearing into the watery depths and never being seen again. But what if your ship was bewitched, and cursed to sail forever more? That is the fate of the legendary *Flying Dutchman* (known in Dutch as *De Vliegende Hollander*). The origins of this legendary ship are uncertain, but it has featured in operas, plays, paintings and novels ever since it was first described in print in 1790, in *Travels in various part of Europe, Asia and Africa during a series of thirty years and upward* (1790) by John MacDonald.

Once upon a time...
The legend states that the crew of the *Flying Dutchman* might try to send messages to land, or to people long dead, if contacted by fellow sailors who encounter it.

Origins:
One possible explanation for the sighting of 'phantom ships' is the 'Fata Morgana' or superior mirage, an illusion that creates an image of a ship that floats mysteriously above the horizon.

In popular culture:
The interstellar gates in science fiction series *The Expanse* by James S.A. Corey make ships disappear if they pass through too quickly, a phenomenon described as 'going dutchman'.

The Ghosts from A Christmas Carol

On a cold Christmas Eve, Ebenezer Scrooge is woken by the ghost of his late business partner, Jacob Marley. So begins *A Christmas Carol* by Charles Dickens, the beloved ghost story. Marley's ghost, eternally encumbered by heavy chains and boxes, tells Scrooge that he has a chance to avoid the same fate. Marley disappears, to be replaced by three more ghosts, one after the other: the Ghost of Christmas Past, the Ghost of Christmas Present and the Ghost of Christmas Yet to Come. They show a terrified Scrooge scenes from his youth, the Christmas unfolding outside his door and the prospect of his own death going unmourned at a future Christmas. Thanks to their lessons, Scrooge repents and embraces a life of kindness.

Once upon a time…
Dickens often highlighted social injustice in his works, and nowhere more so than in this tale of a miser being offered the chance to make amends for his meanness.

Origins:
A Christmas Carol was published on 19 December 1843, and the first printing of 6,000 copies had sold out by Christmas Eve.

In popular culture:
In the 1992 film *The Muppet Christmas Carol*, Michael Caine starred as Scrooge and the puppets Statler and Waldorf played the ghosts of 'Marley and Marley'.

Scrooge's unpleasant meeting with the Ghost of Marley is shown here in this sketch by Arthur Rackham.

"Look to see me no more; and look that, for your own sake, you remember what has passed between us!"

— Charles Dickens, A Christmas Carol

"'Poor, poor Ghost,' she murmured;
'Have you no place where you can sleep?'"

– *Oscar Wilde*, The Canterville Ghost

The tale of the Canterville Ghost has been retold many times, including a 1944 film starring Charles Laughton and Margaret O'Brien.

The Canterville Ghost

In the first of Oscar Wilde's stories to be published, Mr Hiram B. Otis, American Minister to the Court of St James, needs a comfortable home in England for his family and Canterville Castle seems to fit the bill perfectly. When the previous owner warns that the castle is haunted, Mr Otis says he'll take the ghost along with the furnishings. The family soon encounter the mournful ghost of Sir Simon de Canterville, whom the young Otis twins persecute with booby traps. Fifteen-year-old daughter Virginia, however, sympathises with his sleepless plight and helps him find eternal rest at last in the Garden of Death.

Once upon a time…
Oscar Wilde's portrayal of the Canterville Ghost subverts expectations, by showing a ghost who is unable to frighten the residents of his former home.

Origins:
The Canterville Ghost is a short story by Oscar Wilde, which was first published in 1887 in *The Court and Society Review*.

In popular culture:
The story has been adapted for film, television and radio productions all over the world, and it has been the subject of several operas.

Miss Jessel and Peter Quint

Henry James's novella *The Turn of the Screw* opens with a man gathered with friends by the fireside on Christmas Eve. He proceeds to tell the story of his sister's late governess, who took up a post in a country house in Essex in order to care for two young children, Miles and Flora. As the summer unfolded, the governess became aware of the ghostly presences of the previous governess, Miss Jessel, and the gardener Peter Quint, both deceased. She was convinced that the children were aware of them too. The governess's mental health deteriorated and in a shocking ending, Miles died in her arms. Was the late Peter Quint to blame?

Once upon a time…
Although early reviewers saw Henry James's novella as a ghost story, later critics studied the work from a psychoanalytical perspective.

Origins:
The Turn of the Screw is a gothic horror novella by Henry James, first published in serial form in 1898.

In popular culture:
Benjamin Britten's operatic adaptation of *The Turn of the Screw* was first performed in 1954 at the Teatro La Fenice in Venice.

The 1961 film The Innocents, *starring Deborah Kerr, was based on Henry James's horror story* The Turn of the Screw.

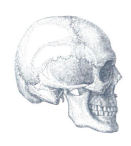

"Peter Quint had come into view like a sentinel before a prison."

– *Henry James,* The Turn of the Screw

"Last night I dreamt I went to Manderley again."

– *Daphne du Maurier,* Rebecca

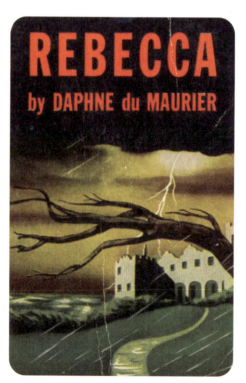

In Daphne du Maurier's novel Rebecca, *the second Mrs de Winter is haunted by the legacy of her late predecessor.*

The 'ghost' of Rebecca

When is a ghost not a ghost? In Daphne du Maurier's novel *Rebecca*, a young woman marries the widowed Maxim de Winter and moves into his grand house in the Cornish estate of Manderley. The housekeeper, a dour Mrs Danvers, does not welcome the new Mrs de Winter, constantly comparing her unfavourably to Maxim's late wife Rebecca. After a campaign of manipulation by Mrs Danvers, Mrs de Winter is so tormented by Rebecca's legacy that she is on the point of killing herself – but the investigation of a shipwreck reveals that all is not as it seems. Rebecca's 'ghost' can no longer hurt her, and neither can Mrs Danvers.

Once upon a time…
Daphne du Maurier does not reveal the name of the second Mrs de Winter, who narrates the book's events, perhaps reflecting the prominence given to her predecessor Rebecca.

Origins:
Rebecca was published in 1938 and sold more than 40,000 copies in its first month on sale.

In popular culture:
Alfred Hitchcock directed a film adaptation of *Rebecca* starring Joan Fontaine and Laurence Olivier, which received the Academy Award for Best Picture in 1940.

Casper the Friendly Ghost

We all know that ghosts are scary – but what if the ghost is a cute little boy who only wants to be friends? Casper, a softly rounded apparition with a friendly face, constantly finds himself accidentally terrifying the people he meets, but always manages to win people over with his generous personality and his bravery. As well as appearing in a long-running series of theatrical cartoons, Casper has also featured in children's books, comics and several films, including the film *Casper* in 1995, which was the first film to have a fully CGI character in a starring role.

Once upon a time...
Caspar's adventures are not confined to Earth: in one episode of the cartoon series, he visits the moon and saves King Luna and his people from an attack by malicious walking trees.

Origins:
Casper is a fictional character who was first featured in 55 cartoon episodes of *The Friendly Ghost* between 1945 and 1959.

In popular culture:
Casper was storyboarded as a character in the animated film *Who Framed Roger Rabbit?*, released in 1988, but he did not make it into the final version.

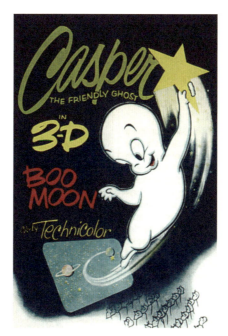

Casper the Friendly Ghost has delighted audiences ever since his first appearance in 1945.

*"Oh, when I was a little Ghost,
A merry time had we!
Each seated on his favourite post,
We chumped and chawed the buttered toast
They gave us for our tea."*

– *Lewis Carroll, 'Phantasmagoria'*

"… Human stories are practically always about one thing, aren't they? Death. The inevitability of death."

– *J.R.R. Tolkien, 1968 BBC interview*

The Dead Men of Dunharrow were freed from their curse by Aragorn, in Tolkien's The Lord of the Rings.

The Dead Men of Dunharrow

he Lord of the Rings by J. R. R. Tolkien has been famous since the first volume of the series was published in 1954, and the film versions only heightened their appeal. Among the vividly drawn cast of hobbits, elves, dwarves, orcs and other terrifying creatures, there also appears an army of dead soldiers, in the fifth of the six books that make up the series. The Dead Men of Dunharrow had, in life, promised to serve King Isildur, but when they betrayed him, they were cursed to live in undying misery. When Aragorn, the rightful heir to Isildur's title, called on them and their king to join him in battle, they were freed from the curse, and crumbled into dust.

Once upon a time…
The Dead Men of Dunharrow dwelled in the Dwimorberg, or Haunted Mountain.

Origins:
The King of the Dead and the Dead Men of Dunharrow are characters in Book V: *The War of the Ring* in J. R. R. Tolkien's fantasy series *The Lord of the Rings*.

In popular culture:
In the 2003 film adaptation of *The Return of the King*, directed by Peter Jackson, the Dead Men of Dunharrow are known as the Army of the Dead.

The Overlook Hotel

fter losing his job as a teacher, Jack Torrance thinks that a winter job as a hotel caretaker will provide a much-needed refuge for him, his wife and their young son Danny, and give them an opportunity to grow closer to each other. But fate has other ideas in Stephen King's famous horror novel *The Shining*. The desolate Overlook Hotel, where Jack and his family now live, is haunted – and Danny is able to see the ghosts, thanks to a special psychic gift known as 'the shining'. The hotel turns its sinister powers on Jack, driving him to madness and violence and, eventually, to his own death.

Once upon a time…
A brief stay at The Stanley Hotel in Estes Park, Colorado, in 1974 inspired Stephen King to create the Overlook Hotel.

Origins:
The Overlook Hotel is the setting for the horror novel *The Shining* by Stephen King, first published in 1977.

In popular culture:
Stanley Kubrick directed and produced a film based on the book, which was released in 1980, starring Jack Nicholson, Shelley Duvall and Danny Lloyd.

These wax figures of the Grady daughters form the film of The Shining *conjure up the terrifying atmosphere of the Overlook Hotel.*

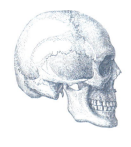

"Monsters are real, and ghosts are real too. They live inside us, and sometimes, they win."

– *Stephen King,* The Shining

The Ghost of Beloved

oni Morrison's award-winning novel *Beloved* is set in Cincinnati, Ohio, in 1873, after the end of slavery in the United States – but the legacy of enslavement shapes the whole book. Sethe, the main character, escaped from slavery in the 1850s with her children. When the manager of the plantation arrived at her house after only 28 days of freedom, Sethe killed her two-year-old daughter, to save her from being returned to slavery, and the manager decided to leave them in Ohio. Sethe could only afford to have one word engraved on her daughter's gravestone: 'Beloved'. Throughout the novel, Beloved makes her presence known, and then arrives as a fully grown woman, before eventually fading back into memory.

Once upon a time...
Beloved was inspired by the true story of Margaret Garner, a woman who escaped enslavement and killed her own daughter rather than see her returned to slavery.

Origins:
Beloved was published in 1987 and was awarded the Pulitzer Prize for Fiction the following year.

In popular culture:
A film version of the book was released in 1998, starring Oprah Winfrey as Sethe and Thandiwe Newton as Beloved.

Toni Morrison's novel Beloved *explores the brutal impact of slavery in the United States.*

"I always know the ending; that's where I start."

– *Toni Morrison,* Every Day a Word Surprises Me & Other Quotes by Writers

"I just thought, "Let's do a comedy ghost movie, but let's base it on the real research."

– *Dan Aykroyd, co-writer,* Ghostbusters

With his insatiable appetite, Slimer causes mayhem at the Sedgewick Hotel in the 1984 film Ghostbusters.

Slimer

host stories often tell of unquiet spirits who hunger for vengeance, but every now and then, we encounter a ghost who is simply hungry for food. Slimer, a blob-shaped green entity, lives in the Sedgewick Hotel in New York, and is never happier than when he's tucking into the delights of an unattended room service trolley. The hotel staff have learned to live with him, and try to keep life as normal as possible for any passing guests, but when the imminent arrival of demigod Gozer the Gozerian leads to increased paranormal energy in the city, Slimer's behaviour becomes harder to cope with, and there's only team that can take on the case: the newly formed Ghostbusters.

Once upon a time...
Slimer was originally known as the 'Onion Head Ghost' by the production team, as his foam-rubber puppet had an unpleasant smell.

Origins:
Slimer is a green ghost with a large mouth, a squishy body and thin arms who first appeared in *Ghostbusters* in 1984.

In popular culture:
In the animated series *The Real Ghostbusters*, Slimer is no longer an antagonist but is now the team's mascot and friend.

The Hogwarts Ghosts

Where would a school of magic be without any ghosts? Luckily, this is not a problem that needs to be solved at the Hogwarts School of Witchcraft and Wizardry in J.K. Rowling's *Harry Potter* novels, because each of the four school houses has its own resident spirit. Gryffindor House is haunted by Nearly Headless Nick, or Sir Nicholas de Mimsy-Porpington as he is more formally known. The ghost of Ravenclaw House is the Grey Lady, the late Helena Ravenclaw, who was murdered by the Bloody Baron – who would himself go on to become the ghost of Slytherin House. Finally, Hufflepuff House is graced by the cheerful spirit of the Fat Friar.

Once upon a time…
In the *Harry Potter* universe, only witches and wizards can become ghosts; muggles (non-magical people) can neither become ghosts nor see them.

Origins:
The Hogwarts ghosts reside in Hogwarts Castle, and each one is the patron ghost of one of the school's four houses.

In popular culture:
The *Harry Potter* novels have become the best-selling book series in history, available in multiple languages all over the world.

*Lady Helena Ravenclaw is just one of the ghostly inhabitants
of Hogwarts School of Witchcraft and Wizardry.*

"*I'm a writer, and I will write
what I want to write.*"

– *J.K. Rowling*

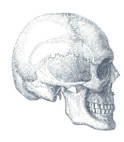

"I find talking about my work harder than it might be if honesty wasn't my calling card."

– *Alice Sebold*

In The Lovely Bones *by Alice Sebold, the ghost of a murdered girl observes the aftermath of her killing.*

Susie Salmon

tories often tell us about the emotional toll of seeing a ghost, but it's rare that we are given the ghost's perspective. In Alice Sebold's novel *The Lovely Bones*, the narrator is a 14-year-old girl, Susie Salmon, who was raped and murdered by a neighbour, George Harvey. From her own personal version of heaven, Susie watches her family and friends as they attempt to cope with their grief. The police are unable to locate her body, and the strain fractures her parents' marriage. Susie is able to briefly connect with a former classmate, Ruth Connors, but otherwise she can only observe events unfolding in the living world.

Once upon a time…
In 2002, Alice Sebold received the Bram Stoker Award for First Novel and the Heartland Prize for *The Lovely Bones*.

Origins:
Susie Salmon narrates Alice Sebold's novel *The Lovely Bones*, telling the story from her perspective as a girl who was raped and murdered and who is now in heaven.

In popular culture:
The Lovely Bones was adapted into a film directed by Peter Jackson in 2009, starring Saoirse Ronan as Susie Salmon.

Picture Credits

Alamy: 21 (Chris Hellier), 33 (Panther Media), 35 (Zoom Historical), 39 (CPA Media), 47 (Penta Springs), 53 (Pacific Press Media), 59 (Jozef Klopacka), 60 (Pawel Kowalczyk), 66 & 69 (Chronicle), 70 (Smith Archive), 75 & 76 (Charles Walker Collection), 83 (Eric Nathan), 87 (Art Collection 2), 88 (The Print Collector), 91 (North Wind Picture Archives), 94 (SuperStock), 97 (Smith Archive), 98 (James Talalay), 105 (Science History Images), 108 (Active Museum), 111 (John Robertson), 114 (David Kilpatrick), 118 (Lankowsky), 121 (World History Archive), 124 (Album), 126 (ClassicStock), 130 (Lebrecht Music & Arts), 133 (Chronicle), 135 (Niday Picture Library), 136 (The Protected Art Archive), 139 (IanDagnall Computing), 140 (Album), 143 (Camerique), 144 (Retro AdArchives), 151 (Yuri Turkov), 153 (Science History Images), 158 (Everett Collection)

Amber Books: 15, 30

Dreamstime: 50 (Darkbird77), 55 (Lario Tus)

Mary Evans Picture Library: 79, 80

Getty Images: 56 (SasinT Gallery), 101 (Quavondo), 117 (Guillame Souvant), 122 (Design Pics Editorial), 147 (LMPC)

Library of Congress: 73, 107

Metropolitan Museum of Art, New York: 36

Public Domain: 40, 63, 102, 129

Shutterstock: 8, 11, 12, 17, 18, 22, 25, 26, 29 (Anuta), 43 (JM-MEDIA), 44, 49 (Lario Tus), 65 (Pawel Kowalczyk), 84, 93, 113, 148 (iobard), 154, 157

Decorative alphabet Paseven via Shutterstock

Background illustrations Alisles, Hein Nouwens, Tatiana Sidenko and shahadatarman all via Shutterstock